1 MONTH OF
FREE
READING

at
www.ForgottenBooks.com

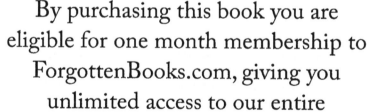

By purchasing this book you are eligible for one month membership to ForgottenBooks.com, giving you unlimited access to our entire collection of over 1,000,000 titles via our web site and mobile apps.

To claim your free month visit:
www.forgottenbooks.com/free1201568

ISBN 978-0-331-50225-1
PIBN 11201568

A THOUSAND OF
THE BEST NOVELS

500

COMPILED BY THE
NEWARK FREE PUBLIC LIBRARY.

NEWARK, NEW JERSEY
1904

1,000 Dec., 1904, Newark, N. J., Library.

500 Dec., 1904, New Jersey Public Library Commission.

2,000 Jan., 1905, Newark, N. J., Library.

1,000 Feb., 1905, Brooklyn, N. Y., Library.

1,000 Feb., 1905, Cossitt Library, Memphis, Tenn.

1,000 Feb., 1905, Washington, D. C., Library.

200 Feb., 1905, Nebraska Public Library Commission.

250 Feb., 1905, Scranton, Wetmore & Co., Rochester, N. Y.

BAKER PRINTING CO.

INTRODUCTION.

Much of the best literature is fiction. Shakespeare's fancy did not burden itself with facts. His history was far less accurate than Winston Churchill's. His imagination waited on his humor, as alway in the fabulist. Dogberry's original would be harder to find than David Harum's. All dramas are novels plus a playright's stage directions. Poetry is fiction first, and then poetry. Chaucer began the great line of English story-tellers; and Hardy and Barrie, and scores of others, are their worthy followers.

If printing was a happy thought and books are not a curse, then novels must be praised. They belong, with the dramas and the poems, among the good things which make our heritage; which unite men by community of thought and feeling; which make it a joy to have the art of reading; and give us simple pleasures, strong emotions, knowledge of our fellows, and sympathy with all mankind.

One may live well and be happy and read no stories; but most are wiser, happier and worth more to their fellows for the novels they have read.

There is much discussion of the novel and most of it quite profitless. To no two men does life seem the same. Each, if he writes, must report that which he sees. One talks of realism, and professes to give us a transcript of life as it truly is; and forgets that the life which truly is, for him, is a life no other ever saw or ever can see, and that his own vision set out in words of his own choosing is a part of his own self, and real to no other mind.

It pleases some to write the fanciful romances. They lay the scene in fairy land, in Caesar's Rome, in Cromwell's England, or in a Kansas country town, as is to them easy and attractive. If well done they seem true to fact as one reads them. They portray men and women who seem like the men and women of our daily experience. Between this good romance and the best of realistic novels, who can draw a line of separation?

And shall the novel have no purpose? May it not try to make a little history more real? To enforce a moral? To plead for some reform? To expose some abuse, gird at some folly, satirize some weakness? To these questions the sufficient answer is the abounding fact. If trees may grow and birds may sing then novels may be as their writers please. Moreover, supply follows demand. Many like their history, sermons, satires, psychology, and all their studies of their fellowmen set forth in fiction, and dramas, poetry and the novel are straightway produced. Why quarrel with this? And why beat the air with a vain discussion of forms, influences and rules and principles? Tom Sawyer is a good story, but its moral is not easily found. Many have found morals in King Lear, and call it also a good tale. Neither story is true. To say both are realistic makes neither better worth reading. To condemn either because it differs from the other is absurd. To read discussions of either by one less a poet than Shakespeare or less a humorist than Twain is a waste of time.

And yet, some novels are surely better than others, as well as different from them; it is wise to read chiefly the better ones; and how shall we distinguish if one does not compare? Are there not principles of literary criticism which one may learn, and then may apply and then may see fiction humbly classify itself into best, good, poor and bad before one's eyes? Because novels pass from the best to the worst by an infinite series of minute gradations are we estopped from saying of any one, this is in the upper ranks, of another, this is in the lower ranks? Within certain limits, yes. Is there no way of telling a good novel when you see one? No, there is not.

Here are poems, plays and stories. Their prime purpose is to please. If that statement seems to set too high a value on pleasure and to underestimate teaching and preaching, then we can at least say that if novels do not please they are not read and fail at all points. If they please a few, they are in so far good; if they please many we may call them better. How shall we arrive at a more definite estimate? Is the best poet he who is most read? May we insist that in the rating of the poet's work the character of his readers be considered as well as their number? May a poem or a story prove its greatness by its popularity? Does it lose its greatness as its popularity wanes? Have we a supreme court of fiction?

The conclusion of the whole matter is simple.   We cannot make rules for pleasures, or regulate taste by laws.   Tastes, feelings, pleasures come by nature, and they come differently to every one.   They do not come by reason and they do not change to order.   A good general guide in art, in belles-lettres, in fiction, poetry and drama is this: Those things which have pleased the most people for the longest time are the better.   The better book is the one that gives the greater pleasure, and those that have long given pleasure not only deserve praise for work done but deserve to be reported as likely to continue to give pleasure. Further, those persons are likely to be better judges of the pleasure-giving capacities of a book who have read many books, who take delight in reading, and so have shown themselves to be sensitive to such matters as style, plot and characterization.   The old books, then, which have long been read and enjoyed are probably worth reading again.   And of the newer books those are more likely to be worth reading which people with experience, sensitive temperament and brains say are good.

This is a preface to a list of good novels.   The compilers of it have not assumed to be judges; but have selected from the old books those that seem best as judged by their more frequent use by people of taste and sense, and from the newer books those which the best current criticism points out as best worth while. Accordingly, we call it a list of a thousand of the best novels. It has been selected by the best rule we could discover, the rule of experience.

*   *   *   *   *

The library buys some of the new novels as issued from month to month and year to year.   Most of them lose their popularity in a few months.   Copies of them accumulate on the shelves, and the titles swell the catalog.   As they wear out they must be replaced, if still in the catalog; and yet they are little wanted.   To meet these difficulties we propose to revise the whole list, omit those little used, select good editions of the titles remaining on the list thus reduced and try to keep a good supply of them on hand.   The thousand titles herewith form the foundation of such a shortened list.   Not all the other 4000 titles now on the shelves will be dropped; but many of them will be, gradually; some will be transferred to literature, and some will be retained and their cards kept in the catalog. This list meanwhile will be widely circulated, being offered as a sufficiently large collection for ordinary use. New novels will be purchased as issued as heretofore and the thousand titles will be reprinted in about a year, with such omissions and additions as criticism and good new books make advisable .

We have omitted some of those older books which are in every library, which no gentleman's library should be without, which everyone knows of and very few read. It seemed unnecessary to reprint their titles here .

We wished to cover the whole field and have thought it proper to omit a good many titles from the long lists of such acknowledged masters as Scott, Balzac and Hardy and to put in books by lesser men. Thus we may have lowered the grade of the whole a little; but have, we hope, by covering a wider range of writers, made it more interesting.

We have come down to date. And because we wish the list to be attractive to the average reader in the average library, we have admitted a good many recent books whose worth is still open to question.

Books for young people, not popular with the elders, we have reserved for a brief supplementary list. The same is true of fairy tales, folk-lore and books of humor not carrying a strong thread of story .

*   *   *   *   *

On a list of all the novels in the Newark library, about 5000 titles, a D was placed opposite all titles found in the list of about 1800 novels for old and young compiled by the Denver public library in 1896. This Denver list was formed by selecting about half of the 3500 titles which had been purchased by that library during the previous seven years.

On the same list an S was then marked opposite all titles found in a list of novels compiled by the City Library, Springfield, Mass., in 1901. This Springfield list was formed by selecting about 1800 novels for adults from a list of about ten thousand gathered during the previous 40 years.

On the same list an A was then marked opposite all titles found in the list of novels for adults, about 800 titles, forming part of the list of 8000 books for small libraries compiled by the American Library Association for the St. Louis Exhibition. This was done from galley proofs, not from the final list.

Then the librarian, the first assistant, and the chiefs of the reference and delivery departments and the reading room in the Newark library marked, on this same Newark list, their several initials opposite the 1000 titles they each preferred.

The Newark list was then marked in the same way for a thousand titles, by Miss Medlicott, reference librarian of the City Library, Springfield, Mass.

It was then checked by Leypoldt and Iles' list of books for girls and women and their clubs.

With these several marks as a basis, and following them in most cases, the Newark library then selected about 700 titles as a first draft of the final list. To these titles were added full names, publishers and prices.

Most of the marks placed as above described were gathered opposite a total of about 1400 titles. Of these the 700 selected for a basis were only half. It has been interesting to note that the selection of the 300 titles to complete the 1000 was much the more difficult part of the task. It seems that about 700 novels may be classed as obviously "good." We think almost any reader would put about 700 of the books in this list in a list of the thousand best which he might compile. About the other 300, opinions would widely differ.

These 700 were sent, with a note of explanation, to a number of the librarians of the State, with the request that they criticize and add. On the basis of their replies a few titles were dropped from the first 700. From the titles suggested for addition—few in number—and from the rejected 700 of the first 1400, 300 were finally chosen.

The completed list of a thousand titles was then put in type and galley proofs were sent to all those who criticized the first proof, and to several others. A few changes were made on the basis of the criticisms returned with these proofs.

JOHN COTTON DANA.

Newark, N. J., Dec., 1904.

A THOUSAND OF THE BEST NOVELS.

Abbott, C. C. Colonial wooing....................$1.00. Lipp
About, E. F. V. King of the mountains...........$1.00. Rand
  Man with the broken ear.......................$1.00. Holt
  Story of an honest man.......................$.50. Appleton
Ade, George. Artie.............................$1.25. Stone
Aguilar, Grace. Days of Bruce................$1.00. Appleton
Ainsworth, W. H. Old St. Paul's..............$1.25. Scribner
  Tower of London............................$1.50. Appleton
Aldrich, T. B. Marjorie Daw, (stories)......$1.50. Houghton
  Prudence Palfrey...........................$1.50 Houghton
  Stillwater tragedy ....$1.50. Houghton
Alexander, *Mrs. pseud. see* Hector, *Mrs.* Annie F. (T.)
Allen, C. G. B. Miss Cayley's adventures.......$1.50. Putnam
  Tents of Shem ....$.87. Chatto
Allen, J. L. Choir invisible ....$1.50. Macmillan
  Kentucky cardinal..........................$1.00. Harper
  Mettle of the pasture ....$1.50. Macmillan
  Reign of law ....$1.50. Macmillan
Altsheler, J. A. Wilderness road..............$1.50. Appleton
Andersen, H. C. Improvisatore................$1.00. Houghton
  Only a fiddler.............................$1.00. Houghton
Andrews, Mary R. S. Kidnapped colony ....$1.25. Harper
Anstey, F., *pseud. see* Guthrie, T. A.
Arblay, *Mme.* Frances (B.) d'. Evelina. 2v....$2.00. Macmillan
Atherton, *Mrs.* Gertrude (F.) Aristocrats........$1.50. Lane
  The conqueror ....$1.50. Macmillan
Auerbach, Berthold. On the heights. 2v..........$2.00. Holt
  Villa on the Rhine. 2v.....................$2.00. Holt
Austen, Jane. Emma.......................$1.50. Macmillan
  Northanger Abbey ....$1.50. Macmillan
  Pride and prejudice ....$1.50. Macmillan
  Sense and sensibility......................$1.50. Macmillan
Austin, Jane G. Betty Alden.................$1.25. Houghton
  Nameless nobleman ....$1.25. Houghton
  Standish of Standish.......................$1.25. Houghton

Bagot, Richard. Casting of nets...................$1.50. **Lane**

Balestier, C. W. Benefits forgot..............$1.50. **Appleton**

Balzac, Honore *de*. The Alkahest *same as* The Alchemist.

$1.50. **Little**

César Birotteau ....$1.50. **Little**

The Chouans...................................$1.50. **Little**

Country doctor...............................$1.50. **Little**

Cousin Bette ....$1.50. **Little**

Cousin Pons ....$1.50. **Little**

Eugenie Grandet ....$1.50. **Little**

Magic skin ....$1.50. **Little**

Pére Goriot ....$1.50. **Little**

Quest of the absolute.......................$1.50. **Little**

Baring-Gould, Sabine *see* Gould, Sabine Baring—

Barlow, Jane. Irish idylls.......................$2.00. **Dodd**

Kerrigan's quality ....$1.25. **Dodd**

Strangers at Lisconnel ....$1.25. **Dodd**

Barr, *Mrs.* Amelia E. (H.) Bow of orange ribbon..$1.25. **Dodd**

Friend Olivia ....$.75. **Dodd**

Jan Vedder's wife.............................$1.25. **Dodd**

Barr, Robert. In the midst of alarms.............$1.50. **Stokes**

Tekla ....$1.25. **Stokes**

Barrett, Frank. Admirable Lady Biddy Fane......$.87. **Cassell**

Barrie, J. M. Little minister..................$1.50. **Caldwell**

Little white bird............................$1.50. **Scribner**

Sentimental Tommy...........................$1.50. **Scribner**

Tommy and Grizel. *sequel to* Sentimental Tommy.

$1.50. **Scribner**

Window in Thrums.......................$1.25. **Scribner**

Barry, William. New Antigone............$1.25. **Macmillan**

Two standards ....$1.50. **Century**

Bates, Arlo. Pagans........................$1.00. **Houghton**

Baylor, Frances C. Claudia Hyde............$1.25. **Houghton**

On both sides................................$1.25. **Lipp**

Bayly, Ada E. (Edna Lyall). Donovan........$1.00. **Appleton**

In the golden days......................$1.00. **Appleton**

Bazin, René. Blot of ink ....$.87. **Cassell**

Behrens, Bertha (W. Heimburg). Magdalen's fortunes,

$.75. **Fenno**

Bellamy, Edward. Duke of Stockbridge.........$1.50. Scribner
    Looking backward; 2000-1887...............$1.00. Houghton
Benefactress, The. *Anon*.....................$1.50. Macmillan
Benson, B. K. Who goes there?............$1.50. Macmillan
Benson, E. F. Luck of the Vails..............$1.50. Appleton
Besant, Walter. All in a garden fair ....$.87. Chatto
    All sorts and conditions of men..............$1.25. Harper
    Beyond the dreams of avarice................$1.50. Harper
    Children of Gibeon...........................$1.25. Harper
    St. Katherine's by the tower.................$1.25. Harper
       and Rice, James. Chaplain of the fleet......$.62. Chatto
         Golden butterfly ....$.87. Chatto
         Ready-money Mortiboy ....$.62. Chatto
Bierce, Ambrose. In the midst of life [stories]..$1.25 Putnam
Bishop, W. H. House of a merchant prince....$1.25. Houghton
    Writing to Rosina...........................$1.00. Century
Bjornson, Bjornstjerne. Arne.................$1.00. Macmillan
    Fisher-maiden..............................$1.25. Macmillan
Black, William. Daughter of Heth..............$1.25. Harper
    In silk attire................................$1.25. Harper
    Kilmeny ....$1.25. Harper
    Macleod of Dare............................$1.25. Harper
    Princess of Thule...........................$1.25. Harper
Blackmore, R. D. Lorna Doone................$1.00. Harper
    Perlycross ....$1.75. Harper
    Springhaven................................$1.00. Scribner
Boldrewood, Rolf, *pseud. see* Browne, T. A.
Boucicault, Dion *see* Reade, Charles *&* Boucicault, Dion.
Bourget, Paul. Cosmopolis.......................$1.50. Tait
    The disciple ....$1.50. Scribner
    Pastels of men.   2v........................$1.50. Little
Boyesen, H. H. Falconberg..................$1.50. Scribner
Braddon, *Miss, see* Maxwell, *Mrs.* Mary E. (B.)
Bread-winners. *Anon* ....$.75. Harper
Briscoe, Margaret S. Jimty, and others (stories) $1.50. Harper
    Sixth sense, and other stories.................$1.25. Harper
Bronte, Charlotte, *see* Nicholls, *Mrs.* Charlotte (B.)
Broughton, Rhoda. Cometh up as a flower......$1.00. Appleton
    Nancy ....$1.00. Appleton

Brown, Alice. The Mannerings................$1.50. Houghton
  Meadow-grass (stories) ....$1.50. Houghton
  Tiverton tales ....$1.50. Houghton
Brown, John. Rab and his friends (stories)...$1.00. Houghton
Brown, W. G., ed. Gentleman of the South....$1.50. Macmillan
Browne, T. A. (Rolf Boldrewood). Robbery under arms.
                                    $1.25. Macmillan
  Squatter's dream ....$1.25. Macmillan
Brudno, E. S. The fugitive.................$1.50. Doubleday
Brush, Christine C. Colonel's opera cloak.........$1.50. Little
Buchanan, R. W. Master of the mine.............$1.00. Rand
  Shadow of the sword..........................$1.00. Burt
Buerstenbinder, Elizabeth (E. Werner). Alpine fay..$.75. Lipp
  Saint Michael.................................$.75. Lipp
Bulwer-Lytton, E. G. E. L., baron Lytton. Caxtons.
                                    $1.25. Harper
  Harold, the last of the Saxon kings........$1.50. Longmans
  Kenelm Chillingly............................$1.25. Harper
  Last days of Pompeii.........................$1.00. Little
  Last of the barons ....$1.25. Lipp
  My novel. 2v. ....$2.50. Harper
  Paul Clifford ....$1.25. Lipp
  Rienzi.......................................$1.00. Little
Bunner, H. C. Jersey street and Jersey lane.....$1.25. Scribner
  Love in old cloathes, and other stories.......$1.50. Scribner
  Midge...$1.00. Scribner
  Short sixes [stories].........................$1.00. Puck
  Suburban sage ....$1.00. Puck
  Zadoc Pine and other stories.................$1.00. Scribner
Burnett, Mrs. Frances E. (H.) Haworth's......$1.25. Scribner
  In connection with the DeWilloughby claim...$1.50. Scribner
  Lady of quality...............................$1.50. Scribner
  Louisiana ....$1.25. Scribner
  That lass o' Lowrie's.........................$1.25. Scribner
  Through one administration ....$1.50. Scribner
Burnham, Mrs. Clara L. (R.) Dr. Latimer....$1.25. Houghton
  Next door.....................................$1.25. Houghton
Bynner, E. L. Agnes Surriage...............$1.25. Houghton
  Begum's daughter..............................$1.25. Houghton

Cable, G. W. Dr. Sevier......................$1.25. Scribner
    Grandissimes ....$1.25. Scribner
    John March, southerner.................$1.50. Scribner
    Old Creole days........................$1.25. Scribner
Caine, T. H. H. Bondman...................$1.50. Appleton
    Deemster ....$1.50. Appleton
    Manxman ....$1.50. Appleton
    Prodigal son ....$1.50. Appleton
Cambridge, Ada *see* Cross, *Mrs.* Ada (C.)
Carey, Rosa N. Nellie's memories...........$1.00. Lippincott
    Not like other girls....................$1.00. Lippincott
Carryl, G. W. Zut, and other Parisians (stories)
                                            $1.50. Houghton
Caskoden, Edwin, *pseud. see* Major, Charles.
Castle, *Mrs.* Agnes S. *&* Castle, Egerton. Pride of Jennico.
                                            $1.50. Macmillan
    Star dreamer ....$1.50. Stokes
Catherwood, *Mrs.* Mary (H.) Days of Jeanne D'Arc.
                                            $1.50. Century
    Lady of Fort St. John...................$1.25. Houghton
    Mackinac and lake stories...............$1.50. Harper
    Romance of Dollard......................$1.25. Century
    Story of Tonty..........................$1.25. McClurg
Chambers, R. W. Cardigan...................$1.50. Harper
    Lorraine ....$1.25. Harper
    Maids of Paradise.......................$1.50. Harper
    Red Republic............................$1.25. Putnam
Charles, *Mrs.* Elizabeth (R.) Schönberg Cotta family.
                                            $1.00. Dodd
Chatrian, Alexandre *see* Erckmann, Emile *&* Chatrian, Alexan-
    dre.
Cherbuliez, Victor. Count Kostia.............$1.25. Holt
    Samuel Brohl and Company................$1.00. Ormeril
Child, F. S. Colonial witch............$1.25. Baker & Taylor
Cholmondeley, Mary. Danvers jewels and Sir Charles Danvers.
                                            $1.00. Harper
    Red pottage ....$1.50. Harper
Church, A. J. Chantry priest of Barnet.......$1.50. Scribner
Churchill, Winston. The Crisis.............$1.50. Macmillan
    Crossing ....$1.50. Macmillan
    Richard Carvel ....$1.50. Macmillan

Clark, K. E. Dominant seventh.................$.50. Appleton
Clarke, M. A. H. For the term of his natural life.

$1.50. Macmillan
Clemens, S. L. (Mark Twain). Adventures of Tom Sawyer.

$1.75. Harper
  Connecticut Yankee in King Arthur's court....$1.75. Harper
  Huckleberry Finn.............................$1.75. Harper
  Pudd'nhead Wilson ....$1.75. Harper
    and Warner, C. D. Gilded age............$2.00. Harper
Clifford, *Mrs.* Lucy (L.) Aunt Anne...........$1.25. Harper
  Love letters of a worldly woman..............$1.25. Harper
Cody, Sherwin, *ed.* Selections from the world's greatest
        short stories ....$1.00 net. McClure
Coffin, C. C. Daughters of the Revolution.....$1.50. Houghton
Collins, W. W. Armadale.......................$1.25. Harper
  Man and wife.................................$1.25. Harper
  Moonstone ....$1.25. Harper
  New Magdalen ....$1.25. Harper
  Woman in white..............................$1.25. Harper
Coloma, Luis. Currita.........................$1.50. Little
Colton, A. W. Port Argent ....$1.50. Holt
Connolly, J. B. Out of Gloucester [stories].....$1.50. Scribner
Connor, Ralph, *pseud. see* Gordon, C. W.
Conrad, Joseph. Falk.........................$1.50. McClure
  Lord Jim ....$1.50. McClure
  Typhoon ....$1.00. Putnam
Cooke, J. E. Surry of Eagle's Nest.........$1.50. Dillingham
Cooke, *Mrs.* Rose (T.) Happy Dodd.........$1.25. Houghton
  Somebody's neighbors.......................$1.25. Houghton
Cooper, J. F. Leather stocking tales.
        Deerslayer ....$1.25. Macmillan
        Last of the Mohicans ....$1.25. Macmillan
        Pathfinder ....$1.25. Macmillan
  Pilot ....$1.25. Putnam
  Spy ....$1.00. Putnam
  Water witch................................$1.25. Putnam
  Wing-and-wing ....$1.25. Putnam
Coppée, F. E. J. The rivals...................$.50. Harper
  Ten tales ....$1.25. Harper

Corelli, Marie. "Ardath"..........................$1.00. Rand
   Romance of two worlds.....................$1.00. Rand
   Thelma ....$1.00. Rand
Cotes, *Mrs.* Sarah J. (D.) Social departure....$1 75. Appleton
   Those delightful Americans....................$1.50. Appleton
Couch, A. T. Quiller-. Astonishing history of Troy Town.
                                        $1.25 Scribner
   Dead man's rock.............................$1.25. Scribner
   Delectable Duchy ....$1.25. Scribner
   Hetty Wesley ....$1.50. Macmillan
   Ship of stars ....$1.50. Scribner
   Splendid spur ....$1.25. Scribner
Craddock, Charles Egbert, *pseud. see* Murfree, Mary N.
Craigie, *Mrs.* Pearl (R.) (John Oliver Hobbes). Robert Orange.
                                        $1.50. Stokes
Craik, *Mrs.* Dinah M. (M.) John Halifax, gentleman.
                                        $.90. Harper
   Noble life ....$.90. Harper
Crane, Stephen. Red badge of courage.........$1.00. Appleton
Crawford, F. M. Cigarette maker's romance..$1.50. Macmillan
   Corleone. 2v. *Sequel to* Don Orsino.......$1.50. Macmillan
   Don Orsino. *Sequel to* Sant 'Ilario.......$1.50. Macmillan
   Mr. Isaacs ....$1.50. Macmillan
   Paul Patoff ....$1.50. Macmillan
   Pietro Ghisleri ....$1.50. Macmillan
   Sant 'Ilario. *Sequel to* Saracinesca........$1.50. Macmillan
   Saracinesca ....$1.50. Macmillan
Crockett, S. R. Gray man.....................$1.50. Harper
   Raiders ....$1.50. Macmillan
   Stickit minister ....$1.50. Macmillan
Cross, *Mrs.* Ada (C.) Three Miss Kings......$1.00. Appleton
Cross, *Mrs.* Mary A. (E.) L. (George Eliot). Adam Bede.
                                        $1.00. Little
   Daniel Deronda ....$1.00. Little
   Felix Holt, the radical......................$1.00. Little
   Middlemarch ....$1.00. Little
   Mill on the floss...........................$1.00. Little
   Romola ....$1.00. Little
   Scenes of clerical life......................$1.00. Little
   Silas Marner ....$1.00. Little

Curtis, G. W. Prue and I.......................$1.50. **Harper**
Cutting, Mary S. Little stories of married life..$1.25. McClure
Daskam, Josephine D. Madness of Philip......$1.50. McClure
Daudet, Alphonse. Jack. 2v..............$2.00. Macmillan
  Kings in exile.............................$1.00. Macmillan
  La Belle Nivernaise and other stories.........$.75. Crowell
Davis, R. H. Exiles, and other stories..........$1.50. Harper
  Gallagher, and other stories.................$1.00. Scribner
  Soldiers of fortune ....$1.50. Scribner
  Van Bibber and others.......................$1.00. Harper
Davis, *Mrs*. Rebecca B. (H.) Doctor Warrick's daughters.
                                        $1.50. Harper
Davis, W. S. Friend of Caesar..............$1.50. Macmillan
Deland, *Mrs*. Margaret W. (C.) Dr. Lavendar's people.
                                        $1.50. Harper
  John Ward, preacher ....$1.25. Houghton
  Old Chester tales............................$1.50. Harper
  Philip and his wife.........................$1.25. Houghton
DeMille, James. Dodge club ....$.60. Harper
  Strange manuscript found in a copper cylinder. $1.25. Harper
Dickens, C. J. H. Bleak House..............$1.00. Macmillan
  Christmas carol .....:.....................$.60. Houghton
  Cricket on the hearth ....$.60. Houghton
  David Copperfield ....$1.00. Macmillan
  Dombey and son ....$1.00. Macmillan
  Great expectations ....$1.50. Scribner
  Nicholas Nickleby ....$1.00. Macmillan
  Oliver Twist ....$1.00. Macmillan
  Our mutual friend ....$1.00. Macmillan
  Pickwick papers ....$1.00. Macmillan
  Tale of two cities...........................$1.50. Scribner
Disraeli, Benjamin, *earl of Beaconsfield*. Coningsby..$1.00. Dodd
  Lothair ....$.60. Longmans
Dix, Beulah M. Blount of Breckenhow........$1.00. Macmillan
  Making of Christopher Ferringham.......$1.50. Macmillan
    and Harper, C. A. Beau's comedy.......$1.50. Harper
Dostoyeffsky, F. M. Crime and punishment..... ..$1.00. Lane
Dougall, Lily. Beggars all...................$1.00. Longmans
  Mormon prophet ....$1.50. Appleton
Douglas, Amanda M. Hope Mills................$1.50. Lee

Doyle, A. C. Adventures of Sherlock Holmes....$1.50. Harper
    Micah Clarke ....$1.75. Harper
    Refugees ....$1.75. Harper
    Sign of the four..........................$1.50. Lippincott
    White company ....$1.75. Harper
Dragomanoff, Michael (Stepniak). Career of a nihilist.
                                            $.75. Harper
Drew, Catharine. Lutaniste of St. Jacobi's........$1.00. Holt
Dudevant, *Mme*. Amantine L. A. (D.) (George Sand). Fadette.
                                            $1.00. Little
    Fanchon, the cricket......................$1.00. Peterson
    Haunted pool. *Same as* Devil's pool...........$1.25. Dodd
    Master mosaic-workers ....$1.25. Little
    Snow man ....$1.50. Little
Dumas, Alexandre. Lady with the camellias........$.60. Hurst
Dumas, A. D. Black tulip......................$1.00. Little
    Chevalier de Maison Rouge.....................$1.00. Little
    Count of Monte Cristo........................$1.50. Crowell
    D'Artagnan romances.
        Three musketeers............................$1.50. Crowell
        Twenty years after. *Sequel to* Three musketeers.
                                            $1.50. Crowell
        Vicomte de Bragelonne. 6v. in 3. *Sequel to* Twenty years
            after ....$3.00. Little
    Valois romances—
        Marguerite de Valois ....$1.50. Crowell
        Chicot the jester ....$1.25. Little
        Forty-five guardsmen........................$1.50. Crowell
DuMaurier, G. L. P. B. Peter Ibbetson.........$1.50 Harper
    Trilby ....$1.75 Harper
Duncan, Norman. Dr. Luke of the Labrador......$1.50. Revell
    The way of the sea..........................$1.50. McClure
Duncan, Sarah J. *see* Cotes, *Mrs*. Sarah J. (D.)
Dunton, T. Watts-. Aylwin......................$1.50. Dodd
Durand, *Mme*. Alice M. C. H. (F.) (H. Greville). Dosia.
                                            $.85. Jenkins
Earle, Mary T. Man who worked for Collister....$1.25. Small
Ebers, G. M. Bride of the Nile...............$1.00. Appleton
    Egyptian princess ....$1.00. Appleton
Eckstein, Ernst. Monk of the Aventine..........$1.00. Little

Edgeworth, Maria. Castle Rackrent, and The absentee.
$1.50. Macmillan
Edwards, Amelia B. Barbara's history ....$.62. Hurst
Eggleston, Edward. Circuit rider...............$.75. Scribner
  Hoosier school-master ....$1.50. Judd
Eliot, George, *pseud. see* Cross, *Mrs.* Mary A. (E.) L.
Elizabeth and her German garden. *Anon*.....$1.75. Macmillan
Elliott, Sarah B. Jerry...........................$1.25. Holt
Erckmann, Emile & Chatrian, Alexandre. Conscript of 1813.
$1.25. Scribner
  Friend Fritz ....$1.25. Scribner
  Madame Therese ....$1.25. Scribner
  Story of a peasant. 2v....................$1.25. Ward, Lock
Ewing, *Mrs.* Juliana H. (G.) Jackanapes..........$.50. Little
  Story of a short life............................$.50. Little
Farjeon, B. L. Blade o'grass................$1.50. Hutchinson
  Joshua Marvel ....$.90. Harper
Fawcett, Edgar. House at High Bridge.......$1.50. Houghton
  New York family...............................$1.00. Cassell
Fenn, G. M. Parson o' Dumford.................$.25. Munro
Fernald, C. B. The cat and the cherub (stories)..$1.50. Century
  Under the jackstaff ....$1.25. Century
Ferrier, Susan E. Marriage. 2v..............$2.00. Macmillan
Feuillet, Octave. Romance of a poor young man....$1.00. Page
Field, Eugene. Little book of profitable tales.....$1.25. Scribner
Field, Roswell. Bondage of Ballinger...........$1.25. Revell
Fielding, Henry. Tom Jones.................$2.00. Macmillan
Fisher, Frances C. (Christian Reid.) Picture of Las Cruces.
$1.00. Appleton
Flaubert, Gustave. Salammbô................$1.50. Doubleday
Fleming, George, *pseud. see* Fletcher, Julia C.
Fletcher, J. S. When Charles the first was king......$.87. Gay
Fletcher, Julia C. (George Fleming). Kismet......$1.00. Little
Foote, *Mrs.* Mary (H.) John Bodewin's testimony.
$1.25. Houghton
  Last assembly ball and Fate of a voice......$1.25. Houghton
  Led-horse claim...............................$1.25. Houghton
Ford, P. L. Honorable Peter Stirling.............$1.50. Holt
Ford, Sewell. Horses nine...................$1.25. Scribner

Fothergill, Jessie. First violin......................$1.00. Burt
   Kith and kin......................................$1.00. Burt
Fowler, Ellen T. Concerning Isabel Carnaby....$1.00. Appleton
   Double thread ....$1.50. Appleton
Fox, John, jr. Cumberland vendetta and other stories.
                                          $1.25. Harper
   Kentuckians ....$1.25. Harper
   Little shepherd of Kingdom Come............$1.50. Scribner
France, J. A. Crime of Sylvestre Bonnard........$.50. Harper
Frankau, Mrs. Julia. Pigs in clover.........$1.50. Lippincott
Franzos, K. E. For the right....................$1.00. Harper
Fraser, Jessie (Tasma). Uncle Piper of Piper's Hill.
                                        .40 pap. Harper
Frederic, Harold. Copperhead.................$1.00. Scribner
   Damnation of Theron Ware....................$1.50. Stone
   In the valley.................................$1.25. Scribner
   March hares ....$1.25. Appleton
   Market-place ....$1.50. Stokes
French, Alice (Octave Thanet). Knitters in the sun.
                                      $1.25. Houghton
   Missionary sheriff ....$1.25. Harper
   Stories of a western town....................$1.25. Scribner
Freytag, Gustav. Debit and credit.............$.60. Harper
   Lost manuscript ....$1.25. Kegan, Paul
Frothingham, Eugene B. Turn of the road.....$1.50. Houghton
Fuller, Anna. Literary courtship ....$1.25. Putnam
   Pratt portraits ....$1.50. Putnam
Fuller, H. B. Chevalier of Pensieri Vani.........$1.25. Harper
   Cliff dwellers ....$1.25. Harper
Gaboriau, Emile. Monsieur Lecoq.............$1.25. Scribner
   Widow Lerouge ....$1.25. Scribner
Garden of a commuter's wife. Anon.........$1.50. Macmillan
Gardner, Sarah M. H. Quaker idylls...............$.75. Holt
Garland, Hamlin. Captain of the Gray-Horse troop.
                                        $1.50. Harper
   Hesper ....$1.50. Harper
   Main-travelled roads, (stories).............$1.50. Macmillan
Gaskell, Mrs. Elizabeth C. (S.) Cranford.....$1.50. Macmillan
Gates, Eleanor. Biography of a prairie girl......$1.50. Century

Gautier, Théophile. Captain Fracasse.............$1.25. Page
 One of Cleopatra's nights, and other fantastic romances.

$1.50. Brentano
 Romance of a mummy.....................$1.25. Lippincott
Gissing, G. R. Our friend the charlatan...........$1 50. Holt
 The Whirlpool ....$1.25. Stokes
Glasgow, Ellen. Voice of the people.........$1.50. Doubleday
Gogol, N. V. Dead souls.......................$1.25. Crowell
 Taras Bulba ....$.60. Crowell
Goldsmith, Oliver. Vicar of Wakefield.......$1.50. Macmillan
Goodwin, *Mrs.* Maud (W.) Four roads to Paradise.

$1.50. Century
 Head of a hundred ....$1.25. Little
 White aprons ....$1.25. Little
Gordon, C. W. (Ralph Connor.) Black rock......$1.25. Revell .
 Man from Glengarry.........................$1.50. Revell
 Sky pilot ....$1.25. Revell
Gould, Sabine Baring-. Broom-squire...........$1.25 Stokes
 Court Royal ....$.50. Smith, E. & Co.
Grahame, Kenneth. Dream days [stories].........$1.25. Lane
 Golden age [stories] ....$1.25. Stone
Grand, *Mme.* Sarah, *pseud. see* McFall, Mrs.
Grant, Charles. Stories of Naples and the Camorra.

$1.75. Macmillan
Grant, Robert. Bachelor's Christmas, and other stories.

$1.50. Scribner
 The undercurrent ....$1.50. Scribner
 Unleavened bread ....$1.50. Scribner
Gras, Felix. Reds of the midi.................$1.00. Appleton
 The terror ....$1.50. Appleton
Greene, *Mrs.* Sarah P. (M.) Cape Cod folks...$1.25. DeWolfe
 Vesty of the Basins.........................$2.00. Harper
Greville, H., *pseud. see* Durand, *Mme.* Alice M. C. H. (F.)
Guthrie, T. A. (F. Anstey). Fallen Idol...........$.75. Lipp
 Tinted Venus ....$1.50. Harper
 Vice-versa ....$1.25. Appleton
Gwynne, Paul. Pagan at the shrine.........$1.50. Macmillan
Gyp, *pseud. see* Martel de Janville, Sybille G. M. A. (deM) *com-
 tesse de.*
 H. *pseud. see* Jackson, *Mrs.* Helen M. (F.) H.

Hackländer, F. W. Behind the counter............$.25. Low
Haggard, H. R. Allan Quartermain.........$1.25. Longmans
   King Solomon's mines.....................$1.25. Longmans
   She ....$1.25. Longmans
Hale, E. E. In His name.......................$1.50. Little
   Man without a country........................$1.50. Little
Halevy, Ludovic. Abbé Constantin.............$1.25. Dodd
   Marriage for love ....$1.25. Dodd
   Parisian points of view.....................$1.00. Harper
Hamblen, H. E. (Frederic Benton Williams). General manager's
   story ....$1.50. Macmillan
   On many seas ....$1.50. Macmillan
Hardy, A. S. But yet a woman...............$1.25. Houghton
   Passe Rose ....$1.25. Houghton
   Wind of destiny...........................$1.25. Houghton
Hardy, Thomas. Far from the madding crowd.. $1.50. Harper
   Mayor of Casterbridge........................$1.50. Harper
   Pair of blue eyes...........................$1.50. Harper
   Return of the native.......................$1.50. Harper
   Tess of the D'Urbervilles....................$1.50. Harper
   Under the greenwood tree....................$1.50. Harper
Harland, Henry (Sidney Luska). As it was written.
                                       $.25. Mershon
   Cardinal's snuff-box ....$1.50. Lane
   Lady paramount ....$1.50. Lane
Harper, C. A., see Dix, Beulah M. & Harper, C. A.
Harraden, Beatrice. Ships that pass in the night..$1.00. Putnam
Harris, J. C. Chronicles of Aunt Minervy Ann..$1.50. Scribner
Harris, Mrs. Miriam C. Rutledge.............$1.00. Houghton
Harrison, Mrs. Burton, see Harrison, Mrs. Constance C.
Harrison, Constance (C.) Anglomaniacs.......$1.25. Century
   Flower de hundred...........................$1.25. Century
Harrison, Mrs. Mary (K.) (Lucas Malet.) Colonel Enderby's
   wife ....$1.00. Appleton
   History of Sir Richard Calmady.................$1.50. Dodd
   Wages of sin.................................$1.50. Fenno
Harte, F. Bret. Colonel Starbottle's client....$1.50. Houghton
   Luck of Roaring Camp and other stories......$1.00. Houghton
   Protégée of Jack Hamlin's and other stories..$1.25. Houghton
   Snowbound at Eagle's ....$1.00. Houghton
   Tales of the Argonauts....................$1.25. Houghton

Hawkins, A. H. (Anthony Hope). Dolly dialogues..$1.50. Holt
  Intrusions of Peggy...........................$1.50. Harper
  Prisoner of Zenda............................$1.50. Holt
  Quisanté ....$1.50. Stokes
  Rupert of Hentzau. *Sequel to* Prisoner of Zenda..$1.50. Holt
  Simon Dale ....$1.25. Stokes
Hawthorne, Nathaniel. Blithedale romance....$2.00. Houghton
  House of seven gables......................$2.00. Houghton
  Marble faun ....$2.00. Houghton
  Mosses from an old manse..................$2.00. Houghton
  Scarlet letter ....$2.00. Houghton
Hay, Mary C. Old Myddleton's money.............$1.00. Burt
Hector, Annie F. (T.) (Mrs. Alexander). Her dearest foe.
                                           $1.00. Burt
  Wooing o't ....$1.00. Burt
Heimburg, W., *pseud see* Behrens, Bertha.
Henderson, C. H. John Percyfield............$1.50. Houghton
Henry, Arthur. Princess of Arcady..........$1.50. Doubleday
Herman, H. *see* Murray, D. C.& Herman, H.
Herrick, Robert. Common lot ....$1.50. Macmillan
Hewlett, Maurice. Forest lovers.............$1.50. Macmillan
  Life and death of Richard Yea and Nay.....$1.50. Macmillan
  Little novels of Italy [stories]..............$1.50. Macmillan
  Queen's quair ....$1.50. Macmillan
Heyse, P. J. L. Children of the world.............$1.25. Holt
  In paradise. 2v...............................$1.50. Appleton
  Romance of the canoness......................$.75. Appleton
Hibbard, G. A. Iduna, and other stories........$1.00. Harper
Hichens, R. S. 'Garden of Allah...............$1.50. Methuen
  Londoners ....$1.50. Stokes
Hickman, W. A. Sacrifice of the Shannon........$1.50. Stokes
Hill, F. T. Minority...........................$1.50. Stokes
  The web ....$1.50. Doubleday
Hillern, Wilhelmina B. *von.* Geier-Wally.......$.60. Appleton
  Higher than the church.........................$.50. Peck
  Only a girl...................................$.75. Lippincott
Hinkson, Katherine (T.) Dear Irish girl......$1.50. McClurg
Hobbes, John Oliver, *pseud. see* Craigie, *Mrs.* Pearl (R.)
Holland, J. G. Arthur Bonnicastle............$1.25. Scribner
  Sevenoaks ....$1.25. Scribner

Holmes, O. W. Elsie Venner.................$1.50. Houghton
    Guardian angel ....$1.50. Houghton
Hope, Anthony, *pseud. see* Hawkins, A. H.
Hopkins, H. M. The torch....................$1.50. Bobbs
Hornung, E. W. Denis Dent ....$1.50. Stokes
    Irralie's bushranger ....$.75. Scribner
    Raffles ....$1.50. Scribner
    Rogue's march ....$1.50. Scribner
Hough, Emerson. Mississippi bubble.............$1.50. Bobbs
Housman, Laurence. Zabrina Warham........$1.50. Macmillan
Howard, Blanche W. Aunt Serena..........$1.25. Houghton
    Guenn ....$1.50. Houghton
    One summer ....$1.25. Houghton
Howe, E. W. Story of a country town........$1.25. Houghton
Howells, W. D. April hopes...................$1.50. Harper
    Chance acquaintance ....$1.50. Houghton
    Hazard of new fortunes.....................$1.00. Harper
    Indian summer ....$1.50. Houghton
    Lady of the Aroostook ....$1.50. Houghton
    Minister's charge ....$1.50. Houghton
    Modern instance ....$1.50. Houghton
    Rise of Silas Lapham......................$1.50. Houghton
Hoyt, Eleanor. Misdemeanors of Nancy......$1.50. Doubleday
Hugo, V. M., *comte.* Man who laughs.........$1.50. Appleton
    Les Miserables ....$1.25. Crowell
    Ninety three ....$1.00. Crowell
    Notre Dame de Paris......................$1.00. Crowell
    Toilers of the sea ....$1.00. Crowell
Hungerford, *Mrs.* Margaret H. Molly Bawn......$1.00. Burt
Hutten, Bettina *von.* Our lady of the Beeches..$1.25. Houghton
    Violett ....$1.50. Houghton
Hyne, C. J. C. Adventures of Capt. Kettle....$1.50. Dillingham
Ingelow, Jean. Off the skelligs..................$1.00. Little
    Sarah de Berenger.........................$1.00. Little
Iron, Ralph, *pseud, see* Schreiner, Oliver.
Irving, Washington. (Geoffrey Crayon.) Rip Van Winkle.
                                       $.75. Putnam
    Sketch book ....$1.50. Putnam
    Wolfert's Roost ....$1.50. Putnam

Jackson, Helen M. (F.) H. Ramona..............$1.50. Little
Jacobs, W. W. At Sunwich port...............$1.50. Scribner
  Dialstone Lane ....$1.50. Scribner
  Many cargoes [stories].......................$1.50. Stokes
James, Henry, *jr.* The American............$2.00. Houghton
  Bostonians ....$1.25. Macmillan
  Daisy Miller ....$1.25. Harper
  Portrait of a lady.........................$2.00. Houghton
  Spoils of Poynton ....$1.50. Houghton
  Washington Square.........................$1.25. Harper
Janvier, T. A. In the Sargasso sea..............$1.25. Harper
  Passing of Thomas, and other stories.........$1.25. Harper
  Stories of old New Spain...................$1.00. Appleton
Jewett, Sarah O. Country doctor............$1.25. Houghton
  Country of the pointed firs.................$1.25. Houghton
  Deephaven ....$1.25. Houghton
  Queenstown [stories] ....$1.50. Houghton
John, Eugenie (E. Marlitt). Gold Elsie..............$.75. Lipp
  Little moorland princess ....$.75. Lipp
  Old mam'selle's secret ....$.75. Lipp
  Second wife ....$.75. Lipp
Johnston, Mary. Audrey ....$1.50. Houghton
  Sir Mortimer ....$1.50. Harper
  To have and to hold ....$1.50. Houghton
Johnston, R. M. Dukesborough tales...........$1.00. Appleton
  Old times in middle Georgia [stories]......$1.50. Macmillan
Jókai, Mór. Black diamonds...................$1.50. Harper
  Eyes like the sea............................$1.00. Putnam
Keary, Annie. Castle Daly.....................$.75. Coates
  Doubting heart ....$1.00. Macmillan
  Janet's home ....$1.00. Macmillan
Keightley, S. R. The cavaliers.................$1.50. Harper
Kernahan, Coulson. Captain Shannon............$.75. Dodd
Kester, Vaughan. Manager of the B. & A......$1.50. Harper
Kettle, Mary S. Rose, shamrock and thistle.....$2.00. Putnam
Kielland, A. L. Tales of two countries..........$1.00. Harper
King, Charles. Between the lines...............$1.25. Harper
  Colonel's daughter ....$1.25. Lipp
King, Grace. Balcony stories...................$1.25. Century

Kingsley, Charles. Hereward, the last of the English.
$1.25. Macmillan
Hypatia ....$1.25. Macmillan
Westward ho! ....$1.25. Macmillan
Kingsley, *Mrs.* Florence (M). Singular Miss Smith
$1.25. Macmillan
Kingsley, Henry. Ravenshoe.................$1.25. Longmans
Recollections of Geoffrey Hamlyn..........$1.25. Longmans
Kipling, Rudyard. "Captains courageous.".....$1.50. Century
Courting of Dinah Shadd, and other stories...$.50. Doubleday
Day's work [stories].......................$1.50. Doubleday
Kim ....$1.50. Doubleday
Many inventions ....$1.50. Appleton
Plain tales from the hills...................$1.50. Doubleday
Soldiers three; The story of the Gadsbys; In black and white.
$1.50. Doubleday
and Balestier, C. W. The Naulahka....$1.50. Doubleday
Kirk, *Mrs.* Ellen W. (O.) Story of Margaret Kent.
$1.25. Houghton
Walford ....$1.25. Houghton
Kirkland, Joseph. Zury ....$1.50. Houghton
Kirschner, Lola, (Ossip Schubin). Erlach court....$.75. Lipp
"O thou, my Austria."........................$.75. Lipp
Korolenko, V. The vagrant (stories)............$.60. Crowell
LaBrete, Jean *de.* My uncle and my curé..........$1.25. Dodd
Lagerlöf, Selma. Story of Gösta Berling.........$1.75. Little
Lamartine, A. M. L. de P. de. Raphael.......$1.00. McClurg
Lane, Elinor M. Nancy Stair.................$1.50. Appleton
Larned, W. C. Arnaud's masterpiece..........$1.25. Scribner
Lathrop, G. P. Gold of pleasure..............$1.00. Lippincott
Lawless, *Hon.* Emily. Grania................$1.00. Macmillan
Lawrence, G. A. Guy Livingstone.............$1.50. Harper
Lee, Mary C. In the cheering-up business.....$1.25. Houghton
Quaker Girl of Nantucket...................$1.25. Houghton
Lever, C. J. Charles O'Malley. 2v..............$3.00. Little
Harry Lorrequer ....$1.00. Little
Maurice Tiernay ....$2.00. Little
Tom Burke of "Ours." 2v.....................$1.00. Burt

Lewis, A. H. The boss......................$1.50. **Barnes**
  Wolfville nights ....$1.50. **Stokes**
Lié, Jonas. Pilot and his wife..................$1.50. **Scott**
Lindau, H. G. P. (Paul Lindau). Lace........$1.00. **Appleton**
Linton, *Mrs.* Eliza (L.) Joshua Davidson......$.25. **Methuen**
London, Jack. Call of the wild..............$1.50. **Macmillan**
  Seawolf ....$1.50. **Macmillan**
  Son of the Wolf; tales of the far North.....$1.50. **Houghton**
Long, J. L. Madame Butterfly, and other stories..$1.25. **Century**
  Prince of illusion [and other stories].........$1.25. **Century**
Loti, Pierre, *pseud. see* Viaud, L. M. J.
Lover, Samuel. Handy Andy....................$1.00. **Little**
  Rory O'More.................................$1.00. **Little**
Lummis, C. F. New Mexico David and other stories.
                                   $1.25. **Scribner**
Lush, C. K. Federal judge...................$1.25. **Houghton**
Luska, Sidney, *pseud. see* Harland, Henry.
Lyall, Edna, *pseud. see* Bayly, Ada E.
Lynde, Francis. The helpers.................$1.50. **Houghton**
Maartens, Maarten, *pseud.* Greater glory....$1.50. **Appleton**
  Joost Avelingh ....$1.50. **Appleton**
  My lady nobody ....$1.75. **Harper**
McCarthy, Justin. The dictator.................$1.25. **Harper**
Macdonald, George. Annals of a quiet neighborhood.
                                   $1.50. **Lothrop**
  David Elginbrod ....$1.50. **Lothrop**
  Sir Gibbie ....$1.50. **Lothrop**
  Warlock o' Glenwarlock ....$1.50. **Lothrop**
  Wilfrid Cumbermede.........................$1.50. **Lothrop**
McFall, *Mrs.* (Mme Sarah Grand). Heavenly twins.
                                   $1.00. **Cassell**
Mackie, Pauline B. Voice in the desert........$1.50. **McClure**
Maclaren, Ian, *pseud. see* Watson, J. M.
McLean, Sarah P., *see* Greene, *Mrs.* Sarah P. (M.)
McManus, L. Silk of the kine.................$1.00. **Harper**
MacManus, Seumas. Through the turf smoke [stories].
                                   $.75. **McClure**
MacQuoid, Katherine S. At the Red Glove.......$1.50. **Harper**
Magruder, Julia. Princess Sonia...............$1.25. **Century**

Major, Charles (Edwin Caskoden). When knighthood was in
    flower ....$1.50. Bobbs
Malet, Lucas, *pseud. see* Harrison, Mrs. Mary (K.)
Mallock, W. H. Human document.............$.87. Chapman
Malot, Hector. No relations.....................$.40. Holt
Margueritte, Paul & Margueritte, Victor. The disaster.
                                       $1.50. Appleton
Marlitt, E. *pseud. see* John, Eugenie.
Marryat, Frederick. Japhet in search of a father.$1.00. Appleton
    Mr. Midshipman Easy.......................$1.00. Appleton
Marshall, *Mrs.* Emma (M.) Under Salisbury spire..$1.25. Seeley
Martel de Janville, Sybelle G. M. A. (de R. de M.) *comtesse de*
    (Gyp). Chiffon's marriage ....$.50. Stokes
Martin, *Mrs.* George M. Emmy Lou..........$1.50. McClure
Mason, A. E. W. Four feathers.............$1.25. Macmillan
    The truants ....$1.50. Harper
Matthews, J. B. Vignettes of Manhattan........$1.50. Harper
Maupassant, H. R. A. Guy de. Modern ghosts....$1.00. Harper
    Odd number; thirteen tales ....$1.00. Harper
    Pierre and Jean ....$.87. Heinemann
Maxwell, Mrs. Mary E. (B.) (Miss Braddon). Aurora Floyd.
                                       $.62. Simpkin
    Fenton's quest ....$.62. Simpkin
    Lady Audley's secret ....$.62. Simpkin
Melville, G. J. Whyte- Gladiators...........$1.25. Longmans
Melville, Herman. Typee ....$1.25. Estes
Meredith, George. Beauchamp's career........$1.50. Scribner
    Diana of the crossways ....$1.50. Scribner
    Egoist ....$1.50. Scribner
    Ordeal of Richard Feverel..................$1.50. Scribner
    Rhoda Fleming ....$1.50. Scribner
Mérimée, Prosper. Carmen ....$2.00. Little
    Columba ....$.60. Longmans
Merriman, Henry Seton, *pseud. see* Scott, H. S.
Merwin, Samuel. His little world..............$1.25. Barnes
    Whip hand ....$1.50. Doubleday
Michelson, Miriam. In the bishop's carriage......$1.50. Bobbs
    The Madigans ....$1.50. Century
Miller Alice D. Calderon's prisoner...........$1.50. Scribner

Mitchell, J. A. Amos Judd......................$.75. Scribner
  Pines of Lory ....$1.50. Life Pub. Co.
  Villa Claudia ....$1.50. Life Pub. Co.
Mitchell, S. W. Adventures of Francois.......$1.50. Century
  Hugh Wynne. 2v.........................$1.50. Century
Montresor, Frances F. At the cross roads......$1.00. Appleton
  Into the highways and hedges...............$1.00. Appleton
Moore, F. F. Jessamy bride.....................$1.50. Stone
Moore, George. Evelyn Inness.................$1.50. Appleton
  Sister Teresa. *Sequel to* Evelyn Inness.........$1.50. Lipp
Morier, James. Adventures of Hajji Baba of Ispahan.
                                $1.50. Macmillan
Morris, William. News from nowhere.........$.60. Longmans
Mulock, Dinah M., *see* Craik, *Mrs.* Dinah M. (M.)
Murfree, Mary N. (Charles Egbert Craddock). In the Tennes-
    see mountains [stories].................$1.25. Houghton ·
  Prophet of the great Smoky mountains.......$1.25. Houghton
  Where the battle was fought................$1.25. Houghton
Murray, D. C. Aunt Rachel..................$1.00. Macmillan
    and Herman, H. The Bishop's Bible......$.87. Chatto
Murray, W. H. H. Adirondack tales...........$1.50. DeWolfe
Needell, *Mrs.* J. H., *see* Needell, *Mrs.* Mary A. (L.)
Needell, *Mrs.* Mary A. (L.) Stephen Ellicott's daughter.
                                $1.00. Appleton
Nicholls, *Mrs.* Charlotte (B.) Jane Eyre........$1.00. Harper
  The professor ....$1.00. Harper
  Shirley ....$1.00. Harper
  Villette ....$1.00. Harper
Noble, Annette L. Uncle Jack's executors.......$1.00. Putnam
Norris, Frank. Man's woman.................$1.50. Doubleday
  Moran of the Lady Letty...................$1.00. Doubleday
  The Octopus ....،.......$1.50. Doubleday
  The Pit ....$1.50. Doubleday
Norris, W. E. Heaps of money.................$.62. Smith
  His grace ....$.50. Street
  Matrimony ....$.62. Smith
Ohnet, Georges. Dr. Rameau.................$.75. Lippincott
  Ironmaster ....$1.50. Rand

Oliphant, *Mrs.* Margaret O. (W.) Chronicles of Carlingford.
   Little pilgrim ....$.75. Little
   Miss Marjoribanks ....$.87. Blackwood
   Perpetual curate ....$.87. Blackwood
   Salem chapel ....$.87. Blackwood
Ollivant, Alfred. Bob, son of battle.........$1.25. Doubleday
Osbourne, Lloyd, *see* Stevenson, R. L. B. & Osbourne, Lloyd.
Ouida, *pseud. see* Ramé, Louisa *de la.*
Overton, Gwendolen. Anne Carmel..........$1.50. Macmillan
   Heritage of unrest ....$1.50. Macmillan
Page, T. N. Gordon Keith...................$1.50. Scribner
   In ole Virginia..............................$1.25. Scribner
   Old gentleman of the black stock..............$.75. Scribner
   Red rock ....$1.50. Scribner
Pain, Barry. Stories and interludes.............$1.00. Harper
Parker, Gilbert. Battle of the strong.........$1.50. Houghton
   Pierre and his people.......................$1.25. Macmillan
   Right of way ....$1.50. Harper
   Seats of the mighty........................$1.50. Appleton
   When Valmond came to Pontiac...........$1.25. Macmillan
Parr, Louisa. Dorothy Fox........................$1.50. Lipp
   Loyalty George ....$.87. Macmillan
Paterson, Arthur. Cromwell's own..............$1.50. Harper
Payne, James. Fallen fortunes...................$.50. Chatto
   Lost Sir Massingberd..........................$.87. Chatto
Payne, Will. Mr. Salt......................$1.50. Houghton
Peard, Frances M. Rose-garden.........$.62. Smith, E. & Co.
   To horse and away.......................$1.50. Whittaker
People of the whirlpool. *Anon.*..............$1.50. Macmillan
Perez-Galdos, Benito. Doña Perfecta............$1.00. Harper
Perry, Bliss. Plated city.....................$1.25. Scribner
Phelps, Elizabeth S., *see* Ward, *Mrs.* Elizabeth S. (P.)
Phillips, D. G. Golden fleece.................$1.50. McClure
   Master rogue ....$1.50. McClure
Phillpotts, Eden. Children of the mist.........$1.50. Putnam
   Sons of the morning........................$1.50. Putnam
Poe, E. A. Tales............................$1.25. Century
Pool, Maria L. Against human nature..........$1.25. Harper
   Mrs. Keats Bradford. *Sequel to* Roweny in Boston.
                                                 $1.25. Harper
   Roweny in Boston...........................$1.25. Harper

Porter, Jane. Scottish chiefs......................$1.00. **Rand**
    Thaddeus of Warsaw ....$1.00. **Rand**
Porter, Rose. Modern Saint Christopher.......$1.25. **Randolph**
Post, W. K. Harvard stories...................$1.00. · **Putnam**
Prince, *Mrs.* Helen C. (P.) Story of Christine Rochefort.
                                        $1.25. **Houghton**
Pushkin, Alexander. Prose tales..............$1.00. **Macmillan**
Quiller-Couch, A. T., *see* Couch, A. T. Quiller-
Ramé, Louisa *de la* (Ouida). Bébée............$.75. **Lippincott**
    Dog of Flanders..................................$.50. **Lipp**
    Strathmore ....\.....................$.75. **Lippincott**
    Under two flags................................$1.00. **Burt**
Raymond, W. Tryphena in love..............$.75. **Macmillan**
Reade, Charles. Christie Johnstone..............$1.00. **Dodd**
    Cloister and the hearth......................$1.25. **Scribner**
    Griffith Gaunt ....$1.25. **Scribner**
    Hard cash ....$1.25. **Scribner**
    It is never too late to mend.................$1.25. **Scribner**
    Peg Woffington ....$1.25. **Scribner**
    Put yourself in his place....................$1.25. **Scribner**
        and Boucicault, Dion. Foul play.........$1.25. **Scribner**
Reid, Christian, *pseud. see* Fisher, Frances C.
Rhoscomyl, Owen. Jewel of Ynys Galon......$1.25. **Longmans**
Rice, *Mrs.* Alice C. (H.) Lovey Mary..........$1.00. **Century**
    Mrs. Wiggs of the cabbage patch.............$1.00. **Century**
Rice, James, *see* Besant, Walter & Rice, James.
Richards, *Mrs.* Laura E. (H.) Mrs. Tree..........$.75. **Estes**
Ridge, W. P. Breaker of laws...............$1.50. **Macmillan**
    Son of the state...............................$1.25. **Dodd**
Ritchie, Mrs. Annie I. (T.) Miss Angel..$1.50. **Smith, E. & Co.**
    Old Kensington ....$1.50. **Smith, E. & Co.**
    Village on the cliff ....$1.50. **Smith, E. & Co.**
Roberts, C. G. D. Forge in the forest.............$1.50. **Page**
    Heart of the ancient wood.....................$1.50. **Page**
Roberts, Margaret. Noblesse oblige..............$1.50. **Harper**
    On the edge of the storm......................$.87. **Warne**
Roberts, Morley. Rachel Marr ....$1.50. **Nash**
Robins, Elizabeth (C. Raimond). Magnetic north..$1.50. **Harper**
    Open question ....$1.50. **Stokes**
Roche, J. J. Her majesty the king..............$1.25. **Badger**

Rohlfs, *Mrs.* Anna K. (G.) Hand and ring.....$1.00. Putnam
    Leavenworth case ....$1.25. Putnam
Ruffini, G. D. Doctor Antonio..............$1.50. Dillingham
Runkle, Bertha. Helmet of Navarre...........$1.50. Century
Russell, W. C. Marooned.......................$1.00. Rand
    My Danish sweetheart......................$.60. Harper
    Sailor's sweetheart..................$1.25. New Amsterdam
    Wreck of the "Grosvenor."......................$1.00. Burt
Sand, George, *pseud. see* Dudevant, *Mme.* Amantine, L. A. (D.)
Sandeau, L. S. J. Catherine...................$1.25. Cupples
Scheffel, J. V. *von.* Ekkehard....................$1.25. Holt
Schreiner, Olive (Ralph Iron). Story of an African farm.
                                  $.60. Little
Schubin, Ossip, *pseud. see* Kirschner, Lola.
Schultz, Jeanne. Story of Colette..............$1.50. Appleton
Scott, H. S. (Henry Seton Merriman). Barlasch of the Guard.
                                  $1.50. McClure
    Last hope....................................$1.50. Scribner
    Sowers ....:..........$1.25. Harper
    With edged tools.............................$1.25. Harper
Scott, Michael. Cruise of the "Midge." 2v.....$2.00. Lippincott
    Tom Cringle's log ....$1.40. Scribner
Scott, *Sir* Walter. Antiquary.................$1.00. Houghton
    Guy Mannering ....$1.00. Houghton
    Heart of Mid-lothian ....$1.00. Houghton
    Ivanhoe ....$1.00. Houghton
    Kenilworth ....$1.00. Houghton
    Old Mortality ....$1.00. Houghton
    Peveril of the Peak ....$1.00. Houghton
    Pirate ....$1.00. Houghton
    Quentin Durward ....$1.00. Houghton
    Rob Roy ....$1.00. Houghton
    Talisman ....$1.00. Houghton
    Waverly ....$1.00. Houghton
    Woodstock ....$1.00. Houghton
Seawell, Mollie E. History of Lady Betty Stair.
                                    $1.25. Scribner
    Sprightly romance of Marsac ....$1.25. Scribner
Sedgwick, Anne D. Paths of judgment........$1.50. Century

Serao, Matilde. Conquest of Rome..............$1.50. Harper
　Land of Cockayne.........................$1.50. Harper
Shackleton, Robert. Great adventurer.......$1.50. Doubleday
Shaw, G. B. Cashel Byron's profession........$1.25. Brentano
　Unsocial socialist ....$1.25. Brentano
Sheehan, P. A. My new curate.................$1.50. Marlier
Sheppard, Elizabeth S. Charles Auchester. 2v..$1.50. McClurg
　Counterparts. 2v.........................$1.50. McClurg
Shorthouse, J. H. John Inglesant.............$1.00. Macmillan
　Sir Percival ....$.87. Macmillan
Sienkiewicz, Henryk. Deluge. 2v. *Sequel to* With fire and
　　　　sword ....$3.00. Little
　"Quo Vadis" ....$1.50. Little
　With fire and sword.........................$1.50. Little
Slosson, *Mrs.* Annie (T.) Fishin' Jimmy.......$1.00. Scribner
　Seven dreamers ....$1.25. Harper
Smith, A. C. Turquoise cup (stories)..........$1.25. Scribner
Smith, F. H. Caleb West, master diver.......$1.50. Houghton
　Colonel Carter of Cartersville...............$1.25. Houghton
　Day at Laguerre's and other days...........$1.25. Houghton
　Fortunes of Oliver Horn....................$1.50. Scribner
　Tom Grogan ....$1.50. Houghton
Snaith, J. C. Mistress Dorothy Marvin........$1.00. Appleton
Spearman, F. H. Nerve of Foley and other railroad stories.
　　　　　　　　　　　　　　　$1.25. Harper
Spielhagen, Friedrich. Hammer and anvil...........$.50. Holt
　Problematic characters ....$.50. Holt
Spofford, *Mrs.* Harriet E. (P.) Amber gods and other stories.
　　　　　　　　　　　　　　　$1.00. Holt
Stael-Holstein, *Mme.* Anne L. G. (N.) Corinne.
　　　　　　　　　　　　　$1.00 net. Macmillan
Steel, *Mrs.* Flora A. (W.) On the face of the waters.
　　　　　　　　　　　　　$1.50. Macmillan
　Potter's thumb ....$1.50. Harper
Stepniak, *pseud. see* Dragomanoff, Michael.
Stevenson, *Mrs.* Fanny V. de G., *see* Stevenson, R. L. B. *&* Stev-
　enson, *Mrs.* Fanny V. de G.
Stevenson, R. L. B. David Balfour.............$1.50. Scribner
　Island nights entertainments ....$1.25. Scribner
　Kidnapped ....$1.50. Scribner

Stevenson, R. L. B. Master of Ballantrae.......$1.50. Scribner
   Merry men, and other tales and fables............$.75. Burt
   New Arabian nights ....$1.25. Scribner
   Prince Otto ....$1.00. Scribner
   St. Ives ....$1.50. Scribner
   Strange case of Dr. Jekyll and Mr. Hyde......$1.00. Scribner
   Treasure Island ....$1.00. Scribner
      and Osbourne, Lloyd. Ebb-tide.........$1.25. Scribner
   The wrecker ....$1.50. Scribner
      and Stevenson, *Mrs.* Fanny V. de G. Dynamiter.
                                           $1.25. Scribner
Stimson, F. J. Guerndale.....................$1.25. Scribner
Stockton, F. R. Adventures of Captain Horn....$1.50. Scribner
   Casting away of Mrs. Lecks and Mrs. Aleshine
                                           $1.50. Century
   House of Martha ....$1.25. Scribner
   Lady or the tiger? and other stories..........$1.25. Scribner
   Late Mrs. Null ....$1.25. Scribner
   Rudder Grange.............................$2.00. Scribner
   Squirrel inn ....$1.25. Century
Stories by American authors. 10v..........$.75 each. Scribner
Stories by English authors. 10v............$.75 each. Scribner
Stories by foreign authors. 10v............$.75 each. Scribner
   French. 3v.
   German. 2v.
   Italian. 1v.
   Polish, Greek, Belgium, Hungarian. 1v.
   Russian. 1v.
   Scandinavian. 1v.
   Spanish. 1v.
Stowe, *Mrs.* Harriet E. (B.) Oldtown folks..$1.50. Houghton
   Sam Lawson's Oldtown fireside stories......$1.50. Houghton
   Uncle Tom's Cabin ....$1.50. Houghton
Stuart, Ruth McE. Carlotta's intended, and other tales.
                                           $1.50. Harper
   Moriah's mourning, and other half-hour sketches.
                                           $1.25. Harper
   Sonny ....$1.00. Century
Sudermann, Herman. Dame Care...............$1.00. Harper
   Regina ....$1.50. Lane

Sue, M. J. *called* Eugene. Mysteries of Paris......$1.25. Burt
  Wandering Jew ....$1.25. Burt
Sullivan, T. R. Day and night stories. 2v......$2.00. Scribner
Suttner, *Frau* Bertha (K.) "Ground arms."......$.75. McClurg
Tarkington, Booth. Gentleman from Indiana...$1.50. McClure
  Monsieur Beaucaire ....$1.25. McClure
Tasma, *pseud. see* Fraser, Jessie.
Tautphoeus, Jemina M. *Freiherrin von.* The Initials. 2v.
                                      $2.50. Putnam
  Quits ....$1.00. Lipp
Taylor, Bayard. Story of Kennett...............$1.50. Putnam
Tchernuishevsky, N. G. Vital question.........$1.25. Crowell
Thackeray, W. M. Adventures of Philip......$1.00. Macmillan
  Henry Esmond ....$1.00. Macmillan
  Newcomes ....$1.00. Macmillan
  Pendennis ....$1.00. Macmillan
  Vanity fair ....$1.00. Macmillan
  Virginians ....$1.00. Macmillan
Thanet, Octave, *pseud. see* French, Alice.
Thompson, Maurice. Alice of old Vincennes......$1.50. Bobbs
Thurston, *Mrs.* Katherine C. The Circle.........$1.50. Dodd
  Masquerader ....$1.50. Harper
Tiernan, *Mrs.* Mary F. (S.) Homoselle...........$.75. Fenno
Tincker, Mary A. Signor Monaldini's niece........$1.00. Little
Todd, Margaret G. Way of escape............$1.50. Appleton
Tolstoy, L. N., *count.* Anna Karenina..........$1.50. Crowell
  Master and man ....$.75. Appleton
  Resurrection ....$1.50. Dodd
  War and peace. 4v. in 2.....................$3.00. Crowell
Tourgee, A. W. Bricks without straw............$1.50. Fords
  Fool's errand ....$1.50. Fords
Tracy, Louis. Wings of the morning.............$1.50. Clode
Trollope, Anthony. Barchester towers ....$.37. Longmans
  Dr. Thorne ....$1.00. Lane
  Framley parsonage ....$.87. Smith, Elder
  Last chronicle of Barset ....$1.75. Smith, Elder
  Small house at Allington.................$.87. Smith, Elder
  Phineas Finn ....$.75. Amsterdam
Truscott, L. P. Mother of Pauline............$1.50. Appleton

Turgénief, I. S. Fathers and sons...........$1.25. Macmillan
    Smoke ....$1.25. Macmillan
    Virgin soil. 2v..........................$2.50. Macmillan
Turner, G. K. The Taskmasters...............$1.25. McClure
Tuttiett, Mary G. (Maxwell Grey). Silence of Dean Maitland.
                                             $1.00. Appleton

Twain, Mark, *pseud. see* Clemens, S. L.
Valdés, A. P. Sister Saint Sulpice..............$1.50   Crowell
Valera, Juan. Dona Luz......................$1.00. Appleton
Van Dyke, H. J., *jr.* Blue flower, and other stories.
                                             $1.50. Scribner
    Ruling passion ....$1.50. Scribner
Verga, Giovanni. House by the medlar tree......$1.00. Harper
    Cavalliera Rusticana ....$.50. Page
Verne, Jules. Around the world in eighty days......$1.00. Burt
    From the earth to the moon.................$2.00. Scribner
    Michael Strogoff ....$.50. Low
    Mysterious island ....$1.00. Burt
    Twenty thousand leagues under the sea..........$1.00. Burt
Viaud, L. M. J. (Pierre Loti.) Iceland fisherman.$1.00. McClurg
    My brother Yves.............................$1.12. Vizetelly
Vielé, H. K. Last of the Knickerbockers..........$1.50. Stone
    Myra of the pines ....$1.50. McClure
Voynich, *Mrs.* Ethel L. (B.) The gadfly...........$1.25. Holt
    Olive Latham ....$1.50. Lippincott
Waineman, Paul. By a Finnish lake............$1.50. Methuen
Walford, *Mrs.* Lucy B. (C.) Baby's grandmother.
                                             $1.00. Longmans
    Mr. Smith ....$1.00. Longmans
Wallace, Lew. Ben Hur ....$1.50. Harper
    Fair god ....$1.50. Houghton
Ward, *Mrs.* Elizabeth S. (P.) Doctor Zay....$1.25. Houghton
    Friends; a duet ....$1.25. Houghton
    Singular life ....$1.25. Houghton
    Story of Avis ....$1.50. Houghton
Ward, *Mrs.* Humphrey, *see* Ward, *Mrs.* Mary A. (A.)
Ward, *Mrs.* Mary A. (A.) Eleanor.............$1.50. Harper
    Lady Rose's daughter ....$1.50. Harper
    Marcella ....$1.00. Macmillan

Robert Elsmere ....$1.25. Macmillan
Sir George Tressady. 2v...................$2.00. Macmillan
Warman, Cy. Tales of an engineer............$1.25. Scribner
Warner, C. D. Golden house. *Sequel to* Little journey in the
    world ....$2.00. Harper
    Little journey in the world....................$1.50. Harper
    That fortune. *Sequel to* The golden house....$1.50. Harper
Waterloo, Stanley. Story of Ab.............$1.50. Doubleday
Watson, J. M. (Ian Maclaren.) Beside the bonny brier bush.
                                      $1.25. Dodd
Webster, H. K. Roger Drake.................$1.50. Macmillan
Webster, H. K. *&* Merwin, Samuel. Calumet "K."
                                    $1.50. Macmillan
    The short line war........................$1.50. Macmillan
Wells, D. D. Her ladyship's elephant..............$1.25. Holt
    The time machine...............................$.75. Holt
Wells, H. G. War of the worlds...............$1.50. Harper
Werner, E., *pseud. see* Buerstenbinder, Elizabeth.
Westcott, E. N. David Harum.................$1.50. Appleton
Weyman, S. J. Gentleman of France.........$1.25. Longmans
    House of the wolf.........................$1.25. Longmans
    Long night ....$1.50. McClure
    Memoirs of a minister of France............$1.25. Longmans
    Story of Francis Cludde....................$1.25. Longmans
    Under the red robe........................$1.25. Longmans
Wharton, *Mrs.* Edith (J.) Greater inclination (stories).
                                    $1.50. Scribner
    Sanctuary ....$1.50. Scribner
    The touchstone ....$1.25. Scribner
    Valley of decision........................$1.50. Scribner
Whitby, Beatrice. Awakening of Mary Fenwick.$1.00. Appleton
    Mary Fenwick's daughter. *Sequel to* Awakening of Mary Fen-
        wick ....$1.00. Appleton
White, Eliza O. Browning courtship, and other stories.
                                    $1.25. Houghton
    John Forsyth's aunts ....$1.50. McClure
White, S. E. Blazed trail....................$1.50. McClure
    Silent places ....$1.50. McClure
Whiteing, Richard. No. 5 John St.............$1.50. Century

Whitlock, Brand. 13th district...................$1.50. Bobbs
Whitney, *Mrs.* Adeline D. (T.) Ascutney street.
                                        $1.25. Houghton
   Golden gossip ....$1.25. Houghton
   Real folks ....$1.25. Houghton
Wiggin, *Mrs.* Kate D. (S.) Cathedral courtship and Penelope's
       English experiences ....$1.00. Houghton
   Penelope's progress ....$1.25. Houghton
   Rebecca of Sunnybrook farm ....$1.25. Houghton
Wilkins, Mary E. Humble romance and other stories.
                                        $1.25. Harper
   Jane Field ....$1.25. Harper
   Jerome, a poor man ....$1.50. Harper
   New England nun, and other stories..........$1.25. Harper
   Pembroke ....$1.50. Harper
   Portion of labor...........................$1.50. Harper
Williams, Frederic Benton, *pseud. see* Hamblen, H. E.
Williams, J. L. Princeton stories...............$1.00. Scribner
Williamson, C. N. *&* Williamson, *Mrs.* Alice M. (L.) Lightning
   conductor ....$1.50. Holt
   The princess passes ....$1.50. Holt
Wilson, H. L. The spenders ....$1.50. Lothrop
Winthrop, Theodore. Cecil Dreeme...............$.75. Dodd
   John Brent ....$.75. Dodd
Wister, Owen. Lin McLean.....................$1.50. Harper
   Red man and white [stories].................$1.50. Harper
   The Virginian ....$1.50. Macmillan
Wood, *Mrs.* E. P. Danesbury House..............$1.00. Rand
   East Lynne ....$1.00. Rand
Woolson, Constance F. Anne...................$1.25. Harper
   Castle Nowhere ....$1.00. Harper
   East Angels ....$1.25. Harper
   For the major ....$1.00. Harper
   Jupiter lights ....$1.25. Harper
Wyatt, Edith. True love....................$1.50. McClure
Yeats, Sidney Levett-. Honour of Savelli......$1.00. Appleton
Yonge, Charlotte M. Daisy chain............$1.25. Macmillan
   Heir of Redclyffe.........................$1.25. Macmillan
Young, Rose E. Henderson..................$1.25. Houghton
   Sally of Missouri.........................$1.50. McClure

Zangwill, Israel. Children of the Ghetto......$1.50. Macmillan
   Mantle of Elijah.............................$1.50. Harper
   The Master ....$1.75. Harper
Zola, Emile. The Downfall...................$1.50. Macmillan
   Lourdes ....$.87. Chatto
   Paris [a novel]..............................$.87. Chatto
   Truth ....$1.50. Lane

STORIES FOR YOUNG PEOPLE.

Abbot, Alice B. Frigate's namesake...........$1.00. Century
Abbott, Jacob. Franconia stories (10v. in 5).....$5.00. Harper
Adams, W. H. D. Days of chivalry................$.75. Estes
Aguilar, Grace. Days of Bruce................$1.00. Appleton
Aiken, John & others. Eyes and no eyes...........$.20. Heath
Alcott, Louisa M. Eight cousins..................$1.50. Little
    Jack and Jill ....$1.50. Little
    Little men ....$1.50. Little
    Little women ....$1.50. Little
    Under the lilacs ....$1.50. Little
Alden, W. L. Adventures of Jimmy Brown.......$.60. Harper
    Cruise of the canoe club.....................$.60. Harper
    Cruise of the "Ghost."........................$.60. Harper
    Moral pirates. ....$.60. Harper
Aldrich, T. B. Story of a bad boy.............$1.25. Houghton
Amicis, Edmondo de. Cuore.....................$.60. Crowell
Andrews, Jane. Seven little sisters.................$.50. Ginn
    Ten boys who lived on the road from long ago to now.
                                          $.50. Ginn
Barbour, R. H. Behind the line................$1.50. Appleton
    Captain of the crew ....$1.50. Appleton
    For the honor of the school..................$1.50. Appleton
Barnes, James. Yankee ships and Yankee sailors.
                                  $1.50. Macmillan
Baylor, Frances C. Juan and Juanita.........$1.50. Houghton
Bennett, John. Master Skylark.................$1.50. Century
Boyesen, H. H. Boyhood in Norway...........$1.25. Scribner
Brooks, E. S. Boy of the first Empire.........$1.50. Century
    Master of the strong hearts...................$1.50. Century
Brooks, Noah. Boy emigrants.................$1.25. Scribner
    Lem ....$1.00. Scribner
Brown, Abbie F. Lonesomest doll.........$.85 net. Houghton

Brown, Helen D. Her sixteenth year, *Sequel to*
  Little Miss Phebe Gay ....$1.00. Houghton
  Little Miss Phebe Gay.....................$1.00. Houghton
  Two college girls ....$1.25. Houghton
Brush, Mary E. Paul and Persis.............$1.00. Lee & S.
Burnett, *Mrs.* Frances E. (H.) Little Lord Fauntleroy.
                                        $1.25. Scribner
Canavan, M. J. Ben Comee.................$1.50. Macmillan
Canfield, H. S. Boys of the Rincon ranch.......$1.00. Century
Catherwood, *Mrs.* Mary (H.) Rocky Fork......$1.50. Lothrop
Church, A. J. Three Greek children...........$1.25. Putnam
Clark, H. H. Admirals' aid....................$1.25. Lothrop
Clemens, S. L. (*Mark Twain*). Huckleberry Finn.$1.75. Harper
  Prince and the pauper........................$1.75. Harper
  Tom Sawyer ....$1.75. Harper
Coolidge, Susan *pseud., see* Woolsey, Sarah C.
Cotes, *Mrs.* Sarah J. (D.) Story of Sonny Sahib.
                                        $1.00. Appleton
Defoe, Daniel. Robinson Crusoe..............$1.50. Macmillan
Deland, Ellen D. Katrina.....................$1.50. Wilde
  Oakleigh ....$1.25. Harper
Dix, Beulah M. A little captive lad..........$1.50. Macmillan
  Soldier Rigdale ....$1.50. Macmillan
Dodge, *Mrs.* Mary E. (M.) Donald and Dorothy $1.50. Century
  Hans Brinker ....$1.50. Scribner
Duncan, Sarah J., *see* Cotes, *Mrs.* Sarah C.
Edgeworth, Taylor & Barbauld. Waste not, want not and other
  stories ....$.20. Heath
Eggleston, Edward. Hoosier school boy........$1.00. Scribner
Eggleston, G. C. Big brother.................$1.25. Putnam
  Wreck of the Redbird........................$1.25. Putnam
Ewing, *Mrs.* Juliana H. (G.) Mary's meadow......$.50. Little
  Six to sixteen ....$.50. Little
French, Allen. Junior cup....................$1.50. Century
French, H. W. Lance of Kanana................$1.00. Lothrop
Garland, Hamlin. Boy life on the prairie......$1.50. Macmillan
Gilliat, Edward. Wolf's head.................$1.50. Dutton
Grant, Robert. Jack Hall....................$1.25. Scribner

Grinnell, G. B. Jack among the Indians *Sequel to* Jack the
young ranchman ....$1.25. Stokes
Jack the young ranchman......................$1.25. Stokes
H. H., *pseud., see* Jackson, Mrs. Helen M. F. (H.)
Hall, Ruth. In the brave days of old..........$1.50. Houghton
Harris, J. C. Little Mr. Thimblefinger........$2.00. Houghton
Henty, G. A. Bonnie Prince Charlie............$1.50. Scribner
Boy knight ....$1.00. Burt
By pike and dyke ....$1.50. Scribner
Lion of St. Mark.............................$1.50. Scribner
Wulf the Saxon ....$1.50. Scribner
Hill, Elizabeth. My wonderful visit.............$1.20 Scribner
Howells, W. D. A boy's town...................$1.25. Harper
Flight of Pony Baker.........................$1.25. Harper
Hughes, Rupert. Dozen from Lakerim, *Sequel to* The Lakerim
athletic club ....$1.50. Century
Lakerim athletic club ....$1.50. Century
Hughes, Thomas. Tom Brown's school days....$.60. Houghton
Jackson, Helen M. (F.) H. Nelly's silver mine.....$1.50. Little
Jefferies, J. R. Sir Bevis............................$.30. Ginn
Jewett, Sarah O. Betty Leicester.............$1.25. Houghton
Betty Leicester's Christmas. *Sequel to* Betty Leicester.
$1.00. Houghton
Kaler, J. O. (*James Otis*). Life-savers..........$1.50. Dutton
Mr. Stubb's brother; *Sequel to* Toby Tyler......$.60. Harper
Toby Tyler ....$.60. Harper
King, Charles. Cadet days.....................$1.25. Harper
Kipling, Rudyard. Captains courageous........$1.50. Century
Kirk, *Mrs.* Ellen W. (O.) Dorothy Deane....$1.25. Houghton
Krause, Lydia F. (*Barbara Yechton*) We ten......$1.50. Dodd
Laurie, André. School-boy days in Russia.........$1.00. Estes
Lillie, *Mrs.* Lucy C. (W.) Nan ....$.60. Harper
Rolf house, *Sequel to* Nan.....................$.60. Harper
Martineau, Harriet B. Crofton boys..............$.30. Heath
Peasant and the prince..........................$.40. Ginn
Martineau des Chesnez, Elizabeth (L.) Lady Green-satin and
her maid Rosette ....$.75. Coates
Matthews, J. B. Tom Paulding.................$1.50. Century
Molesworth, *Mrs.* Mary L. (S.) Carrots......$1.50. Macmillan

Munroe, Kirk. Campmates.....................$1.25. Harper
  Canoemates ....$1.25. Harper
  Dorymates ....$1.25. Harper
  Flamingo feather ....$.60. Harper
  Raftmates ....$1.25. Harper
  Wakulla ....$.60. Harper
Norton, C. L. Jack Benson's log.................$1.25. Wilde
Otis, James, *pseud., see* Kaler, J. O.
Ouida, *pseud., see* Ramé, Louise *de la.*
Packard, Winthrop. Young ice whalers.......$1.20. Houghton
Page, T. N. Among the camps.................$1.50. Scribner
  Two little confederates ....$1.50. Scribner
Phelps, Elizabeth Stuart, *see* Ward, *Mrs.* Elizabeth S. (P.)
Plympton, Almira G. Wanolasset................$1.25. Little
Pyle, Howard. Men of iron....................$2.00. Harper
  Merry adventures of Robin Hood............$3.00. Scribner
  Otto of the Silver hand......................$2.00. Scribner
Ramé, Louise *de la* (*Ouida.*) Bimbi, stories for children.
                                            $.40. Ginn
Raspe, R. E. Baron Munchausen.................$.20. Heath
Ray, Anna C. Teddy, her book...................$1.50. Little
  Teddy, her daughter...........................$1.50. Little
Reid, Mayne. Afloat in the forest.............$.75. Routledge
  Boy hunters ....$.75. Routledge.
Richards, *Mrs.* Laura E. (H.) Captain January.....$.50. Estes
Saintine, J. X. B. Picciola........................$.35. Ginn
Seawell, Molly E. Little Jarvis.............$1.00. Appleton
  Virginia cavalier ....$1.50. Harper
Sewell, Anna. Black beauty.......................$1.25. Page
Shaw, Flora L. Castle Blair......................$1.00. Little
Smith, *Mrs.* Mary P. (W.) Four on a farm.......$1.20. Little
  Jolly good times, or, Child life on a farm......$1.25. Little
  Jolly good times at school....................$1.25. Little
Smith, Nora A. Three little Marys.............$.85. Houghton
Snedden, Genevra S. Docas, the Indian boy.......$.35. Heath
Spyri, Johanna. Heidi.............................$.40. Ginn
  Rico and Wiseli..............................$1.50. De Wolfe
Stanley, H. M. My Kalulu....................$1.50. Scribner
Stockton, F. R. Story of Viteau...............$1.50. Scribner
  What might have been expected..................$.75. Dodd

Stoddard, W. O. Little Smoke................$1.50. Appleton

  Talking leaves ....$.60. Harper

  Two arrows. ....$.60. Harper

  Red mustang ....$.60. Harper

Thaxter, Celia. Stories and poems for children..$1.50. Houghton

Thompson, D. P. Green mountain boys............$1.00. Lee

Thompson, E. E. Seton. Biography of a grizzly..$1.50. Century

  Trail of the Sandhill stag.....................$1.50. Scribner

  Two little savages..........................$1.75. Doubleday

Tomlinson, E. T. Jersey boy in the Revolution. $1.50. Houghton

  Lieutenant under Washington..............$1.20. Houghton

  War of the Revolution series.............$1.50 each. Wilde

    Three colonial boys.

    Three young continentals.

    Two young patriots.

True, J. P. Iron Star ....$1.50. Little

  Scouting for Washington ....$1.50 Little

Twain, Mark, *pseud., see* Clemens, S. L.

Vaile, *Mrs.* Charlotte M. Orcutt girls ....$1.50. Wilde

  Sue Orcutt *Sequel to* The Orcutt girls..........$1.50. Wilde

Ward, Elizabeth S. P. Gypsy series............$.40 each. Dodd

  Gypsy Breynton.

  Gypsy's Cousin Joy.

  Gypsy's year at the Golden Crescent.

  Gypsy's sowing and reaping.

Ward, H. D. New senior at Andover...........$1.25. Lothrop

Warner, C. D. Being a boy...................$.60. Houghton

White, Eliza O. Ednah and her brothers......$1.00. Houghton

  Little girl of long ago......................$1.00. Houghton

  When Molly was six......................$1.00. Houghton

Whitney, *Mrs.* Adeline D. (T.) Summer in Leslie Goldthwaite's

  life ....$1.25. Houghton

Wiggin, *Mrs.* Kate D. (S.) Bird's Christmas carol.

                         $.50. Houghton

  Timothy's quest ....$1.00. Houghton

Woolsey, Sarah C. (*Susan Coolidge*). Eyebright....$1.25. Little

  Katy books ....$1.25 each. Little

    What Katy did.

    What Katy did next.

    What Katy did at School.

Williams, J. L. Adventures of a freshman.......$1.25. Scribner
Wyss, J. D. Swiss family Robinson..............$1.00. Little
Yechton, Barbara, *pseud., see* Krause, Lydia F.
Yonge, Charlotte M. Armourer's prentices....$1.25. Macmillan
  Prince and the page........................$1.25. Macmillan

FOLK LORE, MYTHS AND FAIRY TALES.

Andersen, H. C. Fairy tales ....$1.00. Houghton
   Stories ....$1.00. Houghton
Arabian nights. ....$.60. Houghton
Asbjörnsen, P. C. Fairy tales from the North..$2.00. Armstrong
   Tales from the fjeld ....$1.75. Putnam
Bain, R. N. *tr.* Cossack fairy tales..............$2.00. Stokes
Baldwin, James. The horse fair ....$1.50. Century
   Story of the golden age.......................$1.50. Scribner
Brown, Abbie F. Book of saints and friendly beasts.
                                 $1.25. Houghton
Browne, Frances. Wonderful chair and the tales it told.
                                  $.30. Heath
Church, A. J. Stories of the magicians............$.75. Dodd
Cooke, Flora J. Nature myths..................$.35. Flanagan
Craik, *Mrs.* Dinah M. (M.) (*Miss Mulock*). Adventures of a
   brownie ....$.60. Harper
   Fairy book ....$.90. Harper
   Little lame prince ....$.30. Heath
Dodgson, C. L. Alice's adventures in Wonderland.
                                 $1.50. Macmillan
   Through the looking glass.................$1.50. Macmillan
French, Allen. Sir Marrok....................$1.00. Century
Grimm, J. L. K. & W. K. Fairy tales................$.50. Burt
Harris, J. C. Uncle Remus, his songs and his sayings.
                                 $2.00. Appleton
Hawthorne, Nathaniel. Wonder book and Tanglewood tales.
                                 $.70. Houghton
Holbrook, Florence. Book of nature myths.....$.65. Houghton
Howells, W. D. Christmas every day............$1.25. Harper
Ingelow, Jean. Mopsa the fairy..................$1.25. Little
Jacobs, Joseph, *ed.* Celtic fairy tales...........$1.25. Putnam
   English fairy tales...........................$1.25. Putnam
   Indian fairy tales ....$1.75. Putnam
Keary, Annie & Keary, Elizabeth. Heroes of Asgard.
                                 $.50. Macmillan

Kingsley, Charles.   Heroes ....$1.25.   Macmillan
   Water babies ....$1.00.   Macmillan
Kipling, Rudyard.   Jungle book.................$1.50.   Century
   Just so stories ....$1.20.   Doubleday
   Second jungle book.........................$1.50.   Century
La Motte Fouque, F. H. C., *baron de*.   Undine......$.35.   Heath
Lang, Andrew, *ed*.   Blue fairy book..........$2.00.   Longmans
   Book of romance ....$1.60 net.   Longmans
   Green fairy book ....$2.00.   Longmans
   Red fairy book ....$2.00.   Longmans
   Yellow fairy book.........................$2.00.   Longmans
Macdonald, George.   At the back of the North wind.
                                   $1.00.   Routledge
   Princess and Curdie.   *Sequel to* The Princess and the goblin.
                                   $1.00.   Lippincott
   Princess and the Goblin....................$1.00.   Lippincott
Mulock, Miss, *pseud., see* Craik, Mrs. Dinah M. (M.)
Pyle, Howard.   Pepper and salt.................$1.50.   Harper
   Wonder clock ....$2.00.   Harper
Rabelais, Francois.   Three good giants.......$1.50.   Houghton
Ruskin, John.   King of the golden river............$.20.   Heath
Scudder, H. E., *ed*.   Book of folk stories........$.60.   Houghton
Stockton, F. R.   Fanciful tales ....$.50.   Scribner
   Floating prince and other fairy tales.........$1.50.   Scribner
Swift, Jonathan.   Gulliver's travels ....$.30.   Heath
Thackeray, W. M.   Rose and the ring.............$.25.   Heath
Zitkala-Sa.   Old Indian legends ....$.50.   Ginn

BOOKS OF HUMOR.

Ade, George. Fables in slang....................$1.00. Stone
Alden, W. L. Adventures of Jimmy Brown.......$.60. Harper
Anstey, *pseud., see* Guthrie, T. A.
Bangs, J. K. House-boat on the Styx............$1.25. Harper
Barham, R. H. (*Thomas Ingoldsby*). Ingoldsby legends.
                                          $1.25. Lane
Barr, J., *ed*. Humour of America..............$1.25. Scribner
Bradley, Edmund (*Cuthbert Bede*). Adventures of Mr. Verdant
     Green ....$1.00. Little
Breitman, Hans, *pseud., see* Leland, C. G.
Browne, C. F. (*Artemus Ward.*) Artemus Ward, his book.
                                          $2.00. Dillingham
Bunner, H. C. Made in France..................$1.00. Puck
Burnand, F. C. Happy thoughts..................$1.50. Little
Carroll, Lewis, *pseud., see* Dodgson, C. L.
Calverley, C. S. Verses and fly leaves............$.75. Putnam
Carruth, F. H. Adventures of Jones............$1.00. Harper
Carryl, G. W. Mother Goose for grown-ups.....$1.50. Harper
Clemens, S. L. (*Mark Twain*). Innocents abroad.$2.00. Harper
     Roughing it ....$2.00. Harper
Daudet, Alphonse. Tartarin of Tarascon.....$1.00. Macmillan
     Tartarin on the Alps.......................$1.00. Macmillan
Dodgson, C. L. (*Lewis Carroll*). Hunting of the snark.
                                          $1.00. Macmillan
Dunne, F. P. (*Martin Dooley*). Mr. Dooley in peace and war.
                                          $1.25. Small
Field, Eugene. Sharps and flats. 2v...........$2.50. Scribner
Gilbert, W. S. Bab ballads.....................$1.50. Coates
Guthrie, T. A. (*F. Anstey*). Vice versa.........$1.50. Harper
Hale, Lucretia P. Peterkin papers...........$1.50. Houghton
Harris, J. C. (*Uncle Remus*). Uncle Remus and his friends.
                                          $1.50. Houghton
Harte, Bret, *see* Harte, F. B.
Harte, F. B. Condensed novels...............$1.25. Houghton

Lightning Source UK Ltd.
Milton Keynes UK
UKHW020023181218
334174UK00013B/2104/P